The Greenhills Gang

in Webster's Best Day Ever!

by MACK McEVOY   illustrated by KEVIN McHUGH

Dedicated to my beautiful wife Donna
and my wonderful children Jacob and Myla.
You are collectively my rock and my inspiration.
I love you all more than mere words could ever say.

Thank you for believing in me. x

*'A man travels the world over in search of what he needs,
and returns home to find it'*

George Moore

Webster got up early,

he couldn't sleep a wink,

Feeling so excited

he could hardly even think.

The day had finally come

for him to get his big award,

He'd now be Master of the Web,

respected and adored.

The Greenhills Gang would all be there

to see their tiny mate,

Weave his special magic

and an awesome web create.

No, not an ordinary web,

it had to be the best.

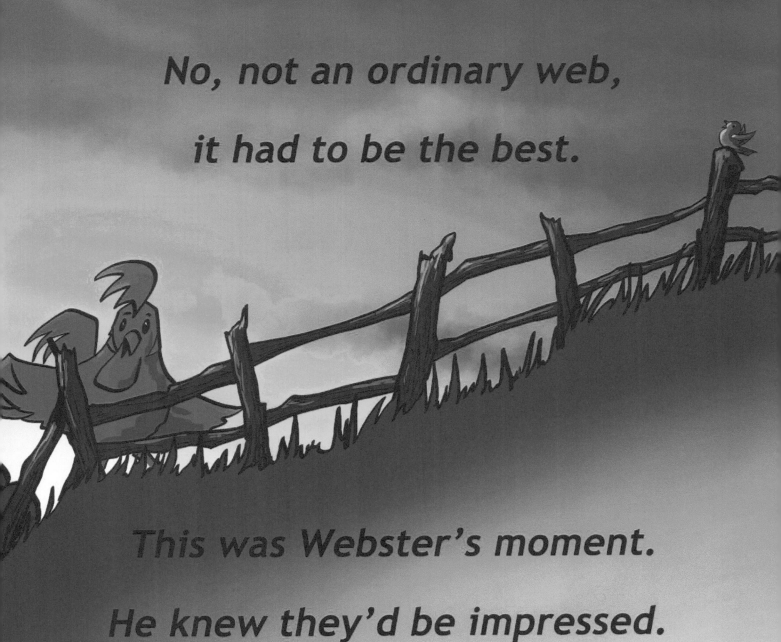

This was Webster's moment.

He knew they'd be impressed.

Millie Moo and Cluxton came,

then

little Whisker

too.

Hamilton and Barkley

soon arrived to join the crew.

So many other animals from far and near showed up

To marvel at his genius and to see him lift the cup.

'Thank you all for coming,'

said Webster with a smile,

'I'll now design a web for you,

it'll only take a while.'

But suddenly he felt quite ill,

his belly in a knot,

No silk would come

and Webster was rooted to the spot.

He felt a panic deep inside

and a wobble in his tummy.

If only he could have a cuddle

from his loving mummy.

Before him were so many eyes

fixed upon him, staring,

Millie Moo
spoke gently,
her voice
so warm and caring.

'Don't you worry, Webster, we know you are the best.

You're simply feeling nervous and perhaps a little stressed.

You don't have to prove yourself in anything you do.

We're your friends and we all love you, simply 'cos you're YOU.

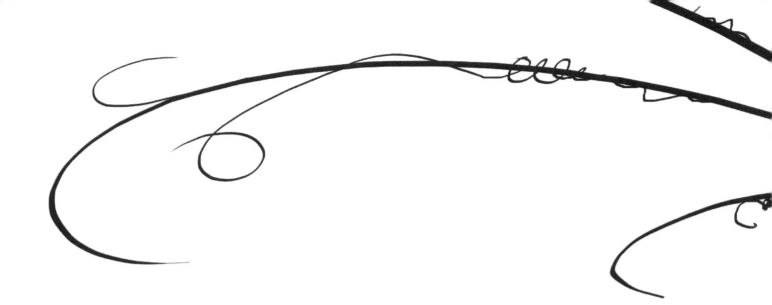

That made Webster feel so great,

his body started humming,

And very soon the special strands

of super silk were coming.

He set to work to weave and stick

and weave and stick some more,

Until he'd built a work of art

from the ceiling to the floor.

With mouths agape the audience

all marvelled at his trade,

As Webster wove a masterpiece,

the finest ever made.

Hopper Green from FARM TV said,

'What a super day!'

He gave the cup to Webster.

The crowd all cheered,

'HOORAY!'

Webster smiled his biggest smile,
the sort that never ends,
He held the trophy high
and shouted,

Published by Making Magic Happen Press,

Perth, WA.

www.mmhpress.com.

National Library of Australia Cataloguing-in-Publisher data:

Juvenille fiction - animals

ISBN (sc) 978-0-6484803-0-3

Printed on sustainable paper.

Lightning Source UK Ltd.
Milton Keynes UK
UKHW050500080223
416583UK00003B/74